Jack Tractor Gets Stuck

Written and illustrated by
Keren Ludlow and Willy Smax

Orion
Children's Books

First published in Great Britain in 1996
by Orion Children's Books
a division of the Orion Publishing Group Ltd
Orion House
5 Upper St Martin's Lane
London WC2H 9EA

Based on a story from JACK TRACTOR
Text copyright © Willy Smax 1995, 1996
Illustration copyright © Keren Ludlow 1995, 1996

The right of Willy Smax and Keren Ludlow to be identified as the author and illustrator respectively of this work has been asserted.

A catalogue record for this book is available from the British Library
Printed in Italy
ISBN 1 85881 286 0

It was early morning. Mike McCannick opened the automatic doors at Smallbills Garage.

"Morning, Benny," said Mike.

"I've got a tough job for you today. Farmer Pyjama wants us to go up to Bedstead Farm. Jack Tractor's stuck in the mud and you've got to help him out."

"That sounds like fun,"
said Benny.

"Wait until you see how deep
the mud is," said Mike.

"If you hurry up you'll be in time for breakfast with the pigs," said Francis.

Benny didn't take any notice. He liked going to Bedstead Farm.

As Benny and Mike drove up to the farm, they saw poor Jack Tractor standing in the duck pond, up to his hubcaps in water.

"What happened?" said Benny.

"My brakes failed as I was coming down the hill," groaned Jack.

"Don't worry," said Benny.
"We'll soon have you out."

Mike fixed Benny's tow-hook to Jack's front axle and Benny began to pull.

Benny pulled and he pulled, but Jack was stuck fast.

Suddenly there was a loud gurgling noise.

Jack shot forward. So did Benny.

BANG!

He crashed
into the
henhouse.

All the hens flew up into the air squawking with fright.

"No harm done," said Farmer Pyjama, and he put the henhouse together again.

Mike dried Jack's spark plugs and topped up his brake fluid.

"Thank you, Mike and Benny," said Farmer Pyjama. "Now we can go and give the pigs their breakfast."

Benny drove back to the garage,
all covered in mud.

"Ha!" said Francis.

"You'll have to have a wash
now, and the water's all cold."

"I don't mind," said Benny.

Suddenly there
was a loud

SQUAWK

and a
big brown
hen flew up
from behind
Benny's cab.

SPLAT! The hen laid an egg on Francis's windscreen.

"Look at that!"
shouted Mike.
"She must have
landed on you
when you crashed
into the henhouse."

"Get it off me!" shrieked Francis.

"Sorry, Francis, I haven't got
time to clean it up now,"
said Mike.
"I'll have to take
this hen back to Bedstead Farm."

And Mike and Benny drove off
down the road, leaving poor
Francis with egg all over his face.